THE
GIRL
AND THE
WOLF

WORDS BY
Katherena Vermette

PICTURES BY
Julie Flett

THEYTUS BOOKS
schchechmala children's series

Cataloguing in Publication information available from Library and Archives Canada

978-1-926886-54-1 (hardcover)

Simultaneously published in Canada and the United States in 2019
Library of Congress Control Number: 2018954133

Summary: This picture book for young children is an empowering Indigenous twist on a classic wolf narrative.

We acknowledge the support of the Canada Council for the Arts, which last year invested $157 million to bring the arts to Canadians throughout the country. Nous remercions le Conseil des arts du Canada de son soutien. L'an dernier, le Conseil a investi 157 millions de dollars pour mettre de l'art dans la vie des Canadiennes et des Canadiens de tout le pays. We acknowledge the support of the Province of British Columbia through the British Columbia Arts Council.

Author photo by KC Adams
Illustrator photo by Courtney Molyneaux

Theytus Books
theytus.com

Printed and bound in Canada.

23 22 21 20 • 6 5 4 3

For Ruby Daawnis
—K.V.

For Amiel, Autumn and Sage
—J.F.

*In loving memory of
Dr. Greg Younging. Maarsii.*

The girl ran through the bush while her mother picked berries. She was helping but mostly running.

"Don't go too far," her mother called. "It's going to be dark soon."

"Okay," the girl said but kept running.

Suddenly the girl looked up and couldn't see her mother anymore.

She panicked and looked one way but didn't see her.

She tried to calm down and looked the other way but still couldn't see her.

Everything got quiet
and dark.
The girl felt cold
and scared.
She didn't know what to do.

Out from between the trees, a tall grey wolf with big white teeth appeared.

The girl was very still.

"What are you doing out here by yourself?" asked the wolf.

"I lost my mother," she said. "I can't see my way back."

"You must be scared, little one," said the wolf in a quiet voice.

"Yes, I am," the girl told him.

"Do you know the way back?" he asked.

The girl shook her head.

The wolf came up close and sniffed her.

His wolf breath was hot and stank of meat.

"I think I know where you come from, little one," said the wolf. "But it is almost dark. You must be hungry."

"Yes, I am." The girl nodded, and her stomach rumbled.

"Do you know how to hunt?" asked the wolf.

The girl shook her head.

"What are you going to do?" asked the wolf.

The girl looked around.
Everything was quieter
and darker.
The girl felt very cold
and very scared.
"I don't know," she said sadly.

"Yes you do," the wolf told her. "Take a deep breath. Close your eyes, then look. What do you see?"

The girl did what he said, and when she opened her eyes she saw something that made her feel better.

"I can eat those berries. They are safe to eat. The ones by the stream where the water is safe to drink." She pointed.

"That's good, little one," said the wolf. "Let's go."

The girl drank in gulps and ate two handfuls of berries.

"Now what are you going to do?" asked the wolf.

The girl looked around.

Everything was still quiet and pretty dark.

"I don't know," she said sadly.

"Yes you do," the wolf told her. "Take a deep breath. Close your eyes, then look. What do you see?"

The girl did what he said, and when she opened her eyes she saw something that made her feel better.

"The skinny trees over there! That's where we camped," the girl said with a big grin.

The grey wolf nodded and smiled at her with his big white teeth.

The girl started walking but was really running. She ran to the air that smelled like her family.

She laughed out loud and looked to her side, but she did not see the grey wolf anywhere.

She looked one way but didn't see him.

She looked the other way but still couldn't see him.

Just then her mother appeared with her basket full of berries.

"Oh, my girl!" her mother cried. "I told you not to go too far."

"Mama! I was lost and a wolf helped me!" the girl told her.

Her mother was surprised. "A wolf?"

"Yes," the girl said. "He was big and grey. At first I thought he was going to hurt me."

Her mother smiled. "Real wolves can hurt people, but I've heard old stories about wolves who help lost children too."

The girl smiled. She was glad the wolf had been the helping kind.

When they returned to their camp, the girl told everyone about her big adventure and her special wolf.

That night she tied tobacco in red cloth and left it at the bush's edge.

Because she didn't know a better way to say thank you.

AUTHOR'S NOTE

This is a completely made-up story. The girl in her red dress and the wolf who isn't really scary came to me when I was reading a lot of European fairy stories. You know the ones where the wolf is always the bad guy and gets run off (or worse) in the end. I don't know about you, but I found that unfair, and I thought of the other stories I had been told where the wolf wasn't just evil or hungry. That's where this story comes from. It is inspired by traditional stories, yes, but in no way taken from one.

Tobacco is one of the four sacred medicines. It can be enclosed in a tie of cloth, or simply given, in thanks or to ask for something respectfully.

In this story, the girl leaves it in thanks to the wolf for helping her because it really is the best way I can think of to say thank you.

Thank you to all the storytellers who have let me listen and have taught me many things over the years. Thanks, too, to Greg for pulling this one out of the pile of forgotten stories, to David for giving it the once-over and especially to Julie for making this little story truly come alive. Special thanks to all the young persons I have had the honour to sit with and learn from—you lead the way, dear ones. Merci, maarsii, chi miigwech.

KATHERENA VERMETTE is a Métis writer from Treaty One territory in Winnipeg, Manitoba. Her first book, *North End Love Songs*, won the Governor General's Literary Award for Poetry in 2013. Her bestselling novel *The Break* won multiple awards, including the 2017 Amazon.ca First Novel Award. Katherena has also written The Seven Teachings Stories, a series of children's picture books, and A Girl Called Echo, a series of graphic novels for young adults. For more information, visit katherenavermette.com, or follow Katherena on Twitter @katherenav.

JULIE FLETT studied fine arts at Concordia University in Montreal, Quebec, and Emily Carr University of Art + Design in Vancouver, British Columbia. She is a three-time recipient of the Christie Harris Illustrated Children's Literature Prize and the 2017 winner of the Governor General's Award for Young People's Literature—Illustrated Books. Julie is Cree-Métis and currently lives in Vancouver, British Columbia, with her son. For more information, visit julieflett.com. Follow her on Twitter @julie_flett.

Also from award-winning illustrator Julie Flett

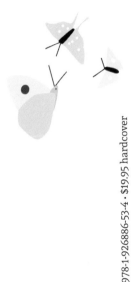

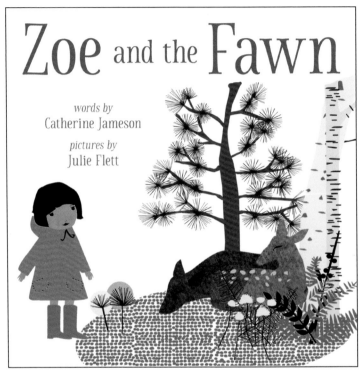

Zoe and the Fawn

words by
Catherine Jameson

pictures by
Julie Flett

978-1-926886-53-4 • $19.95 hardcover